Little Ol' Red Miracle

TAMMY TOMA

Little Ol' Red Miracle

Trilogy Christian Publishers
A Wholly Owned Subsidiary of Trinity Broadcasting Network
2442 Michelle Drive, Tustin, CA 92780

For information about special discounts for bulk purchases, please contact Trilogy Christian Publishing.

Trilogy Disclaimer: The views and content expressed in this book are those of the author and may not necessarily reflect the views and doctrine of Trilogy Christian Publishing or the Trinity Broadcasting Network.

10 9 8 7 6 5 4 3 2 1
Library of Congress Cataloging-in-Publication Data is available.

ISBN 979-8-89333-090-8
ISBN 979-8-89333-091-5 (ebook)

ACKNOWLEDGMENTS

Let your light shine before people, so they can see the good things you do and praise your Father who is in Heaven.

— Matthew 5:16

Miracles happen when God brings people together to help one another in a divine way.

This book is devoted to all the wonderful people who sent prayers, love, and encouragement.

Alyssa and Lola; Daniella and Isa; Megan and Jones; and the motorcross riders—you are amazing human beings! All your heartfelt kindness inspired awe in this beautiful experience!

Thank you to the many *lost pet sites* and beautiful people who sent messages of kindness and advice—I am extremely grateful for all the encouragement and your knowledge.

To the St. Roch Church who prayed with us and all the businesses that hung up flyers, your generosity meant so much.

A big mahalo to Irish Vreeken for the masterclass in editing and Kyle Vreeken for help with the timeline!

Thank you to Aunt Terri and Uncle Tim for helping pass out flyers, the farm sighting, and prayers.

Mahalo to sweet Aunt Amy, Terri, Robby, Ken, and Jenn for your quick tips at any hour during editing.

Uncle Jeff, Aunt Karen, Aunt Bridgette, Aunt Sherry, Aunt Dawn, Aunty Mara, Uncle James, and their families, thank you for the calls and long-distance prayers!

Thank you to Kyle, Mike, Bre, Jansen, Cherise, Ari, Siana, Puni, Kingsley, Maria, Linda M., Kathy S., Laurie, and David for your alerts!

Thank you to my HMK peeps—you guys prayed and cheered for us, and you inspired me much!

I want to thank TBN for believing in miracles. I remember the Crouch family started the channel through a miraculous vision, endurance, and faith. Your ministry has been a major inspiration through many seasons and chapters of my life. Thank you, Trilogy—Lisa, Jason, the graphic and editing teams—you are wonderful! I love working with you!

Thank you, Alan Pineda for the author photo.

Mahalo for your care, Dr. Pressler, Dr. Hancock and team Alii Animal!

DEDICATION

We dedicate this book to our wonderful children—Kenny, Jenn, Robby, Kaui—and their families, our grandchildren, my brother and seven sisters, in-laws, nieces, nephews, cousins, friends, and all our Ohana near and far.

Thank you, Grandma Fran, and Pop-Pop for all your love and faith over the years.

Thank you to my beautiful mother Ellen who taught me the power of prayer, faith, hope, and your endless loving kindness. I miss you and Dad's encouragement, and unending creativity so much. I know you are both watching from Heaven.

We also dedicate this book to our newest family members and all the generations to come.

To the reader of this book, I personally thank God for you and the unique gifts you bring to the world.

— Tammy T

CHAPTER 1

An Island Christmas

Four Weeks Before Christmas

The cool breezes were rumbling the coconut tree leaves as the moon peeked through puffy clouds in the evening sky. Dancing moonbeams sparkled across the water greeting the two-lane road along the coastline. On the mountainside, the homes were dressed with twinkling lights, red hibiscus, leafy green garland, and festivity. The small north-shore town had a special feeling of family and faith at the center, especially in the tropical Christmas season.

Just a few days remained in November when Tammy, Ross, their four dogs and two grandkids, Mila, age four, and Jetty, age two, brought in boxes of treasures from the garage to decorate the Christmas tree. Mila checked all the dogs with her plastic doctor kit, as she did every time she visited. She and Jetty opened the boxes of colorful ornaments excitedly. The delicious merriment, churning sea, chilly and salty breeze created a delightful island scene to bring out cozy sweaters, hibiscus tea, hot coco, and cinnamon malasadas.

"Mele Kalikimaka is the thing to say,
on a bright Hawaiian Christmas day.
That's the island greeting that we send to you,
from land where palm trees sway."

Joyfully, Tammy began singing and swaying with the festive TV tunes. A cute group of yellow fluffy puppies ran on the TV screen. Clifford, the oldest dog, crouched down low, growled, and instantly pounced onto the table. He stared at the screen of invaders—challenging them. Cliff looked from the high table perch as the pups ran off the screen. He was so proud that he chased them out of the house and protected his family! With a roar of laughter, Cliff jumped down, pleased with his triumph, and they got back to singing and decorating.

The four dogs were older, ages nine to fourteen. Hadu, their lovable brindle colored pit-bull, Wailea, a big sweet rottweiler, Columbus a gentle small brown dog, and spirited Clifford also known as Cliff, the fourteen-year-old pack leader, curiously smelled the boxes. Cliff's big brown eyes, reddish-brown fur, curly tail, long graceful legs, and floppy ears accented his strong spunky character.

As the leader of his human and dog pack, he proudly served in his watchful role like a soldier. One of his special talents was how he could take charge of any situation. When his big brown eyes spoke, the other dogs followed the order of his stares. Occasionally, Wailea, the rottweiler, wandered off to chase a mongoose, but she always came home. Cliff was watching her because she had a sneaky stare toward the open door. She was about to naughtily run off—and he knew it. As the pack leader, Cliff had to keep her from bolting out the door.

Christmas lights and ornaments spread about the floor gave everyone a job to untangle and a focus on decorating.

Meanwhile, the Hawaiian winds were blowing intensely, and an unusual noise cut through the windy air.

Aunty Tammy thought she heard an animal "YIPE" loudly from the front yard. Running towards the door, Tammy grabbed a whistle from the kitchen. She saw Hadu and Columbus curled up on the floor but did not see Wailea and Cliff. She opened the door and blew the whistle four times. The dogs were trained to come and sit at the sound of four whistles. Hadu and Columbus ran to her and sat down. Another four whistles and Wailea ran from the street and beelined into the house, breathing heavily, then sat by the others.

Clifford's mama, Aunty Tammy, quickly noticed he was missing. *How in the world could Clifford be missing; he is fourteen years old, and he never wandered from our yard*, she thought. *He must have followed Wailea somewhere and must be nearby.* She kept calling his name loudly and clapping because he was partially deaf in one ear. "Clifford!" clap, clap, clap. Then she began whistling loudly, but there was no response.

She looked desperately all around the house and the neighbors' yards for him, but he was nowhere to be seen. She got in her car and drove all over the quaint little seaside town of twinkling lights.

Uncle Ross searched all night on the windy beach, through the rustling bushes and every yard

Confused and with barely any sleep, they searched the entire next day with no sign of their pack leader.

Tammy made waterproof signs for all the light poles with zip lock bags and pleaded for any help on social media. For four days they hung the bagged posters, passed out hundreds of flyers, and contacted the Humane Society and nearby vet offices. Looking desperately for clues everyday resulted with no sightings of their little ol' red boy!

They began to think and hope that a kind family must have taken him in.

CHAPTER 2

Facing Uncertainty One Step at a Time

~ Do Not Be Discouraged ~

Aunty Tammy and Uncle Ross continued wading for clues as the rain drizzled; they put flyers in every mailbox and knocked on doors to ask if anyone saw him. They expanded the search by going down the coast to the surrounding coconut tree lit towns and nearby college campus. Students, families, and businesses posted and shared his photos—it was now over five days with no clues.

Clifford was missing over five days, it was unbearable! Aunty Tammy's heart ached for him. Cliff followed her everywhere, and she missed her sweet, spunky, fun, little ol' red boy.

Remembering his leadership, she hoped and prayed he had the skills to survive as the weather was rainier and windier.

The sixth day drifted by and he was still missing.

Pulling her golden-brown hair off her pretty little face, Mila noticed one of the bagged "lost dog" posters stapled on a light pole. With a sad frown, it sunk in to her that Clifford was still truly missing. She realized he was all alone and cried for him. Later she questioned again, "Why are there so many posters of Cliff?" She got louder, "He has no food! Is he ok? I am so sad; he is in the forest all alone. How can he get home?" Mila shouted.

Her little brother Jetty looked at the freshly printed posters and pointed to Clifford's bed with a certain expression like he missed the ol' boy.

Tammy tried to comfort the grandchildren and whispered, "Hopefully, people will see him from these posters." She gulped in her throat so she would not cry. "Believe and have faith… and we must do our part"—taking a deep breath, she ordered them, "keep putting the posters in the baggies."

LOST DOG

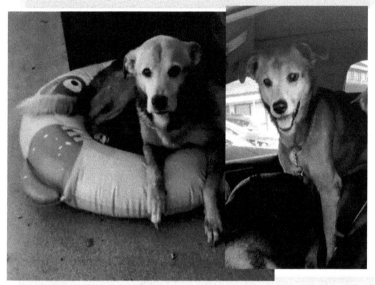

CLIFFORD 14years /40lbs

Partially deaf & cute personality!

Very Spunky & Smart -missing his family
He hears loud claps and whistles.

Lost Dog Poster

CHAPTER 3

Three Weeks Before Christmas

Missing Over One Week

With December inching closer to Christmas, Cliff's disappearance was six days and counting. Feeling like she kept barking up the wrong tree, Aunty Tammy stared at the ceiling quietly praying. "What are we missing?"

Hearing a garbage truck that rolled down the street, she remembered that, in a cruel act, someone dumped a dog at the garbage center because they disliked dogs. A voice or intuition gave her the impression that she should check there. It was a long shot because no one would really dump a dog at the recycle and trash place—would they? Uncertain, she pulled into the long driveway known as "the dump." It was well kept and organized but a place where someone would discard items and trash. She was sure it would be another dead end, but something told her she should try.

To Aunty Tammy's surprise, the dump staffer and the maintenance yard worker both informed her of seeing Cliff two nights earlier—the winter's coldest, rainiest, and windiest evening. Scared for Cliff, they confirmed he looked cold and hungry, but he also ran from them. Cliff was in survival mode, looking for food in the hard rain!

Very far from home, but she finally had a clue! Optimistically happy but confused, she thanked them from the bottom of her heart and gave them her information, asking them to call if he showed up again.

Driving away, she felt an awful sickness in her stomach that someone could have discarded their loveable animal like trash. "The ol' boy is fourteen!" The thought that anyone would be so cruel to him made her skin crawl.

Once the rawness of images in her head calmed, she realized it was a waste of time focusing on her sick feelings and decided to focus on the fact that their dog was somewhere behind the dump. Finding the strength to celebrate the first clue—*the first sighting of Cliff*—they increased the search to the surrounding areas, farms, and local businesses. *"Ding, ding, ding,"* messages were coming in and out of her phone flowing through the island. People showed such care and kindness to look out for Clifford and share his photos.

Aunty Tammy felt that it was almost too painful knowing he was lonely and lost. *Was it possible that he wandered this far?*

He was old and partially deaf. She pondered, *Even though he still has lots of spunk, how did he get over to the dump?*

Reeling in a mixture of thoughts and emotions, she decided to focus like a soldier and carry out the mission to bring Cliff home! With a search and rescue mentality, they gained courage to search harder.

Cliff

CHAPTER 4

Lean into Faith

Two Weeks Before Christmas —
Missing Over Two Weeks

Twelve days passed, and a dog that clearly resembled Cliff was a mile down the road from the dump, deep in the grasslands.

On their last day of vacation, Tammy's twin sister and brother-in-law passed out flyers to beach-goers at nearby beach cabins along the coastal road. "We may have spotted Cliff near the farm—across from the beach," they messaged.

Tammy and Ross eagerly drove to the cabins. *Another clue!* The joy pushed them quicker through the grassy field, but once again he vanished. Tammy noticed her twin sister's face showed they could not secure her little ol boy; he was too far behind two barbed wire fences. Even their loud claps and yells could not get his attention as partially-deaf Cliff ran deeper into the acres of farmland.

Having this new clue added a new location to share with the community and beyond. They had a second clue! *A second sighting of Clifford!*

Locals and more vacationers joined the search party around the farms. One evening, their son from California called that his friends visiting the island heard about the lost ol' boy and wanted to join the search too—*the word was spreading!* Then, while looking out over the water, Tammy and Ross spotted an Iwa bird soaring happily—symbolizing guidance and a pathway home for local fishermen. Could it be a good sign?

Like the ocean waves working tirelessly despite any obstacles, the growing search party kept churning for clues.

During her daily routine of hanging updated flyers around town, some strangers told them to stop putting up posters, saying they should give up.

Trying to be kind but feeling awkward to find words, Tammy breathed in and, shaking it off, said "No, no, no, no…. but thank you, we are anchored in faith." She would not allow a negative thought or comment into the search party's efforts. Using the annoyed feeling for extra fuel, she cranked out one hundred new flyers, and the search party handed them out! Her heart told her that Cliff was searching for them, too! No way were they going to stop now!

Meanwhile, genuine encouragement from many sweet people washed in and nourished her soul.

A nearby church offered to distribute flyers. "How long has he been missing?" a kind lady asked her.

"It has been fourteen days, seven hours, and twenty minutes," she said looking at Cliff's photo on the flyer. Caught off guard when tears instantly flowed from her eyes, she felt embarrassed because she could not stop crying.

Five people in the church surrounded her and said the sweetest prayer. Drawing strength from the divine circle of prayer warriors, Tammy went into soldier mode again and made new strategies.

Every evening, the three animals hopped in the truck with her to place food and stinky socks around the farm entrances while she clapped and whistled. Stinky socks were Cliff's favorite toy, and maybe the scent would draw him out. Hadu, their lovable pit-bull-terrier, ate something by a trash can.

Tammy scolded him loudly, "I DO NOT need a sick dog, why did you eat that!" Hoping he would not get sick, she gave him water and put the three dogs back in the truck to drive and search along the fence line. Columbus began howling because he heard a siren whiz by; then Hadu joined, and Wailea howled as well. The only howl missing was Cliff's. Tammy thought, *Maybe he will hear you?*

At that moment, a smell *so bad* filled the truck. Tammy and Ross flew the windows open.

"See Hadu, now you have a stomach ache, and you are STINKING up the truck! You GOOFY dog! Well—I hope CLIFF CAN SMELL *YOU* FROM HERE!" she yelled—then she began laughing briskly. It was one of the first real laughs she had had for many days—and much needed.

With Christmas approaching, the stress over Cliff's vanished status made them forget to finish decorating the tree. It was hard to feel festive; that ol' boy whom they loved for fourteen years was still missing.

"At least let us see a miracle and spend his senior years together with him," she prayed.

Tammy received continued prayers from the local Church, as well as encouraging messages and prayers from people all over Hawaii and from other states. *For every disappointment, there was a nudge to never quit and to endure.*

One evening, walking Cliff's little brother Columbus, she asked him, "Could we be like two ships passing in the night? Are we nearing each other, but just out of sight?"

Columbus pawed at her, and his little button eyes said, "Let's keep looking down this grassy area."

She remembered Cliff always played a game with his pack where he would lie flat and watch all the other dogs and his family. If a toy or sock landed on the ground, he would slowly walk without detection—snatch the goods—and put them in his bed. The other dogs respected his space and never took his treasures. Hopefully, this skill came in handy the many days and nights he spent alone crouched in the grassy fields. *Maybe he found a safe area to hide with his watchful big brown eyes.* In deep thought, they reached the grassy area Columbus pulled her to, and there was a beautiful sunset.

Now eighteen very long days after Cliff disappeared, Aunty Tammy stared into the vast purple-orange sky and voiced, "I *claim* a miracle breakthrough that we will have a solid sighting or secured capture of Clifford." Aunty Tammy knew in her heart that he was in the area and that he was looking for her and his family too. She prayed. "God, I ask for your help because you, Lord, put it on my heart to keep looking and to endure."

> *You make known to me the path of life; you will fill*
> *me with joy in your presence.*
>
> — Psalm 16:11

CHAPTER 5

Refresh the Soul

Eight Days Before Christmas
— Missing Twenty Days

On Sunday evening, twenty days after Clifford went missing, Ross and Tammy had just finished dinner, and three messages on Aunty Tammy's phone read, "Look at your social media right now!" Her heart pounded with hopeful anticipation as she read the messages. Two sisters hiking one of the tallest mountain peaks found a lost dog below the rushing falls. Taking in a deep breath, she opened another message—and there was Clifford's photo!

Stunned with mixed emotions, they gasped at what they saw with both gladness and concern. Cliff was under leaves, so skinny—and he must have been cold. His sunken eyes looked very weak—not his usual spunky brightness. It WAS their ol' red boy! *Finally, another sighting of Clifford!*

Like a leafy vine, messages grew, adding more clues and information to connect the hikers with Cliff's family.

"I think this is that lost dog Clifford."

"Please contact that lady that's been passing out flyers."

Tammy sent out a reply, "That IS our dog, Clifford! Please help us find this location."

With her confirmation that it was Clifford, messages flowed through the community with joy and anticipation to try to get him home.

The night before, sisters Daniella and Isa had decided they wanted a very challenging hike. They next morning, they hiked up the rough terrain to the North Shore waterfall, spotting a very skinny dog under the rushing waterfall.

They could not believe *this* dog made it to the falls in the highness of *this* mountain! "How could this old, very skinny dog—or *any* dog—get in the bottom of *these* falls?" they pondered. It is a very difficult terrain to hike, and there was only a rope and a flowing rush of water falling over the rocks to enter below where this little old dog was. "Could he have been caught in the flowing falls and ended up riding the surge of water to the bottom? Was there another entrance below?" they asked each other.

"We cannot leave this little old dog alone," both sisters exclaimed at the same time. The sisters decided they would carry him up the rocky wall. Carefully, they zipped up and secured his frail body into their blue backpack.

Cliff was very cooperative and glad of the girls' help. "They are his type of brave heroes," he thought.

Studying the rocky wall, the sisters became determined in their mission. They started the very challenging climb up the rock wall and could feel his little heart beating like a drum. Grasping roots, climbing rope, and—at one point—clawing the wall sideways, they navigated the challenging hike, and his heart continued to *thump, thump*.

Cliff stared down with his wide brown eyes at the water pool he was trapped in. With each step up the rocks, his ears flopped in rhythm. Cliff leaned into the safety of the backpack at each challenge, thinking they were wonderful—and relieved they were helping him.

After the difficult hour to reach the top of the waterfall to a solid path, they were thrilled about the wonderful shared accomplishment and experience! The pup in their backpack had won over their hearts. He was excited and happy at the beautiful view and whimpered that he needed to stretch. The sisters took him out of the blue backpack that carried him to safety, fed him, and shared the special quiet moment. His legs were weak at first, and he wobbled like a newborn puppy before slowly regaining his footing.

Clifford walked with them a few minutes and smelled a familiar scent near the jungled bushes. Without warning, he sprinted off out of sight.

After catching their breath from trying to chase him down, reality set in—he was totally gone. With no words, they stared into openness as a tropical, dirt-filled breeze blew across their faces. They just carried this old pup on their backs, through bamboo, and scaled the rocks with him. Just like that, after all their hard work, he instantly vanished into the mountain brush.

They MUST do something!

Wanting nothing more than to help find the dog's owners, Daniella and Isa posted photos of the brave rescue to a hiking club on social media that started a chain reaction of messages.

Alyssa, a member of the club, happened to be Aunty Tammy's niece. She was excited about the news and sprang into action. Collecting information from the sisters, she connected them with Aunty Tammy.

The heroic sisters could not have imagined that their efforts were now part of the three-week long search party.

Cliff and two brave sisters reached the top of the mountain after the challenging hike out of the falls; Cliff ran off leaving them shocked that they lost him again!

They posted to the local hiking club a photo of Cliff looking sickly. They find a connection to Cliff's family.

Thankfully, Alyssa, Aunty Tammy's niece, is a member of the hiking club and connects her with the two brave hikers. People from all over the country begin sending messages about this difficult hike and offer prayers and share the story. Hundreds of people show such kindness and send encouragement.

CHAPTER 6

Stand Firm in the Tall Mountain

One Week and Four Hours Before Christmas — Missing Twenty Days and Many Hours

It was 8:00 pm; the sky was cloudy and dark when the first message got to Aunty Tammy and Uncle Ross—two hours since the brave sisters alerted the hiking club. Amazed, Tammy talked with the girls and could not believe the heroic efforts they made. Being grateful for bringing Cliff this far, she held in any feelings of panic and stayed focused on the mission. Amid the joy of the news, Tammy and Ross felt the sting that he was once again lost. With a range of emotions, they were glad the sisters cared for him!

Taking in a breath, Ross exclaimed, "That sickly photo of Clifford scared me." And with that, they knew they had to get him out of that mountain tonight and decided to search in the blanket of darkness.

Arriving at the tall, solid land mass in their truck, Tammy asked, "What secret is that dark mountain keeping?"

Ross parked ahead in their small car, jumped out, and eagerly began hiking the dark trail with a headlamp. He braved the wet, slippery mud from the earlier rain, and it almost sucked off one of his shoes. The loud silence amplified the sound of bushes rustling in the wind.

Tammy stayed near the truck with extra lights contacting their sons, who kept alerts that they were safe in the late night.

Ross yelled so much running up the mountain that his throat hurt. A deep darkness swept the mountain; however, Ross could see the trail well with his large range headlamp. Yelling, clapping, and using a whistle to call for Cliff at the top of the mountain path offered nothing—*no sighting*—and he trekked back down the dark mountain frustrated. They were sad and quiet but marched on.

Just as they started to leave, their truck broke down—they could not drive it! The wheels just spun in the mud. A piece under the truck fell off and was no longer connected to shift out the gears. The engine roared loudly with no movement. "What is this? How in the world? Now the truck will not move?" an exhausted thought was all that could be added.

Luckily, they took two cars in case one got locked in the gated area. Tammy stirred up enough energy to find a security guard who kindly comforted them, and he opened the gate for the small car. They had to leave the truck and would worry about that later.

Tammy prayed, "Please God, let this mountain provide Cliff shelter and kindness tonight," and they quietly drove home.

Driving down the dirt road at 10:00 pm, their niece Alyssa alerted them she was in contact with her hiking club members. Leading the charge with her six children, they set up a Command Central to gather information from hikers for the following day! "Clifford is in that area; he is so close to being found!" she messaged to Aunty Tammy who needed the encouraging and kind words.

That evening, Tammy made "Clifford kits" for the hikers with food and other items to coax Cliff to the walking paths. No one was sure which side of the mountain he was on, but everyone involved hoped they could cover it all! The many prayers, kind wishes, and Alyssa's incredible Command Central was going to help!

Trying hard to sleep, they knew they needed energy in the morning for the important mission. At 4:00 am, rain began pattering down, and a veil of worry as cold as the night crept into their minds: "Will Clifford survive the night? His little eyes in the photo looked so sad and malnourished." Quickly pivoting their thoughts, *anchoring in faith*, "However, those sisters did an amazing job carrying him out of the falls; Cliff must be closer to the path." They had to stop worrying and focus on sleeping.

Eating a small breakfast in the car, they reached the hiking entrance at the crack of dawn. Amid the chickens crowing, they divided the landmass strategy. Ross planned to go up the mountain while Tammy planted food, stinky sock pieces, and bed clippings at the bottom in hopes of luring him down to the paths.

Feeling added anxiety, Ross searched frantically because he must catch a flight by 11:00 am—he could not take off work. He yelled desperately, "Cleeeeford, Cleeeeford, Cleeeford," as loud as he could, just as he did the late night before. Clapping and whistling and hoping their little ol' red boy would whimper or show his face. Two hours quickly passed, and Ross hiked down from the mountain—empty handed.

Tammy shared the gloomy and sad look on his face.

The air was still and damp as they quietly talked about next steps. Taking a deep breath, Tammy called the tow truck company to pick up their truck, which was still broken down.

Aunty Tammy and Uncle Ross searched with no sighting of their little ol' boy, and their truck broke down in the dark evening mountain. Tammy reached for strength to get a tow truck to take it out of the mountain.

Little Ol' Red Miracle

CHAPTER 7

Courageous Faith Shines Throughout the Valley

Exactly One Week Before Christmas — Twenty-One Days!

-FAITH CAN MOVE MOUNTAINS-

Tammy stared intensely at the massive mountain, making it clear, "All right, Mountain, this game of hide and seek has been interesting. I am ready to bring Cliff home!" Forming a plan in her mind, she scanned the tall peaks and low valley.

With all that was given so far, she was determined they would find each other that day! The mountain seemed more welcoming as she confidently took on the challenge.

Meanwhile at Alyssa's Command Central, some hikers explained they could not make it because of the rain. The wet trails were difficult and slippery—Tammy understood.

Occasionally, clouds dumped short heavy tropical rains, making Tammy hide in vines and brush just like Cliff probably did. "This must be how Cliff survived these twenty-one days by hiding in the leafy green protection. At least there is fresh water and it is not blistering hot." *She felt so proud of her smart ol' boy.*

Midday messages of encouragement from the community and beyond flooded into Alyssa's Command Central like a waterfall as more hikers said they were on their way. "I am praying hard Aunty! We will find him today! I just received this message from someone asking if it is okay to bring their dogs.

> *Aloha Alyssa—I am Megan. My son Jones and I are heading out in about an hour. Do you think it is okay if I bring my two dogs?*

Tammy responded to Alyssa with an enthusiastic "Yes, that would be wonderful! Please tell her that I am very thankful they are coming!"

This energized Tammy, and she continued calling Clifford's name, clapping loudly, and using the four whistles he was trained to respond to, "Whistle, whistle, whistle, whistle!"

"Vroom, vroom, vroom, vroom," motorcycle sounds echoed in the valley behind Tammy. She waved down two girls on the motorbikes and told them about Cliff's situation.

Being dog-lovers themselves, they jumped at the chance to help. Moments later, they arrived with four riders on motorbikes and their dogs. Adding another divine effort to the mission, they rode up the east ridge, hoping to "encourage the little ol' red boy" down to the path.

That is—IF he was still up on top of the mountain.

Another hour later, the sky dumped rain again and Tammy hid in the bushes like her ol' boy would have. She was missing him dearly, longing for his sweet brown eyes. When the short tropical rain stopped, she thought, "Maybe I should take a break," and began walking out of the trail. Tired but alert, she felt a strong nudge in her soul say, "Go back!" Munching on almond and raisin snack mix, she listened to the nudge and turned back into the trail again.

Walking near the westside mountain path, she saw a white truck with flashing lights and two kind young girls.

"Are you Tammy, Clifford's mom?"

"Yes!" she answered.

The girls were from the Humane Society and decided to hike a different side, the *westside* path, since the motocross bikers went up the *eastside* path—where Cliff ran from Daniella and Isa. Clifford usually hiked with Uncle Ross on that westside path.

"Is it possible that during the night, Cliff's skinny little body could have made it from the east side to the west side?" she questioned.

The two girls went up in their rain gear and great hiking boots!

Marching on, Tammy continued spreading Cliff's food and sock toys, and when one of her shoes got sucked into the mud almost to her shin, she pulled it out of the thickness. "Whistle, whistle, whistle, whistle!"

Moments later, something magical happened. A sweet lady and her son with the brightest smiles walked up with two dogs and said, "Are you Tammy, Alyssa's Aunty?"

"Yes!" It was Megan and her son Jones who had messaged Alyssa they were coming with their dogs to help! As a take-charge, sweet lady, Megan confidently knew what she was going to do with her dogs, then she and Jones headed up the *eastside* path.

Tammy walked back to the front trail, whistling to meet more hikers. She started to cry, thinking of all these kind efforts, all day, and *no sightings*. She prayed harder, "We have come this far, God, it must be today!"

Some hikers messaged Alyssa; they were planning to come the next day! Tammy asked them to try to come now. "I think we have to get him out of this mountain tonight!" Alyssa provided them information, and two more hikers said they were coming.

The motorbikes went silent, stopping for a break.

Little Ol' Red Miracle

The two girls from the Humane Society came down the *westside* path with no sign of Clifford, sadly empty-handed; however, this narrowed the search. Everyone involved could confirm he had to be on that *eastside* path, maybe a mile or so below where the sisters lost him.

Tammy prayed a quiet but firm prayer, "I *claim a miracle* from all these incredible, giving, kind hearts." Marching on, she walked to the bottom field to meet new hikers arriving.

In that moment, Megan and Jones called Tammy. Fumbling through her jacket pockets she pulled out her phone. Staring at the buttons she took a deep hopeful breath and said, "Hello, this is Tammy," and breathlessly waited for a voice.

Megan joyfully exclaimed, "We got Clifford!"

From the bottom of the lush green valley, Tammy finally exhaled and cried with such joy along with Meghan on the phone! She leaned on a nearby coconut tree, sobbing happily. It was such a beautiful moment! The peace and joy in the valley felt as if angels were celebrating and crying with jubilee! Her heart was beating with gratitude and happiness!

Those who refresh others will themselves be refreshed.

— Proverbs 11:25

A patch of bushes and vines made a safe shelter deep off the *eastside* path. Megan and Jones could not have seen it from the trail; however, their dogs surrounded the leafy shelter, and inside, there was skinny little Clifford! Megan's dogs discovered him almost a mile up the eastside path!

Clifford was weak and surely glad to have been rescued; he went onto Jones' shoulders like a shepherd boy!

At the same moment, Aunty Tammy realized the motocross bikers had "encouraged" him down away from the top, closer to the bottom of the *eastside* path!

"IT WORKED... the divine joint efforts of everyone worked! What joy!" she breathed—her heart leapt fully. Again, the peaceful valley felt as if angels were there celebrating all the kind efforts of people helping in big and small ways. Tammy thanked God, remembering her earlier prayer: that the mountain would provide Cliff shelter through the night.

When Alyssa, her husband, and six children saw the message pop up that Clifford was finally found, they danced and cheered the loudest joyful screams filling the Command Central living room. Hundreds of people also celebrated on social media along with them!

Oh, the rejoicing!

Once the hikers handed Clifford to Aunty Tammy, and he realized it was his mama, everyone's eyes filled with tears.

"*Arrrrv OW, ow, yeeeeow; Owwwww, Arrrr aerr, Owowowow,*" Clifford cried and howled and talked in his cries about his experience and lonely nights and his joy—that he was with her again! He was finally going home to his family and his dog pack! "*Ow ow ow yeooo ooooooh, AARRROOOOOW!*"... they all felt that his howls and cries were understood.

The car was familiar, and Alyssa and her children drove up celebrating and singing! They were so excited that they helped their mom organize all the communications! They wanted to see Clifford too at the valley!

With joyful tears, Tammy and Megan hugged and with gratitude-filled hearts, they all celebrated.

Feeling immense joy, Alyssa and Tammy sat with Cliff in her car, and he talked and howled for several minutes. The ol' boy was so happy and relieved after his long journey. Clifford grabbed at the dog food supply Aunty Tammy had been using for twenty-one days.

Watching him eat made her feel happy but also hurt, knowing how many days he had been searching for food. She let him eat small bites and draped a sheet over his skinny back.

Cliff paused and looked up at them with his tired brown eyes with such relief—tears filled their eyes, tugging at their hearts.

Cliff hides in leafy bushes 7 days before Christmas.
21 Days Second Rescue, Halleluiah! — Faith can move mountains

Aunty Tammy finally gets to hold her
Little Ol' Red Miracle after 21 days!
Cliff howls and cries with JOY when he realizes it is her!
He is finally going HOME!

Jones carried him out of the mountain like a shepherd boy — on his shoulders! 1 Week Before Christmas

WOOOOFF, OWOWOWWWO ARRRROWWW!

Megan, Jones, their two dogs — and Tammy filled with joy!

STINKY SOCKS! Cliffs' favorite toy.

CHAPTER 8

Home Is Where the Heart Is!

Seven Days Before Christmas — Evening Sunset after Twenty-One Days

NOW HOME

Aunty Tammy brought the ol' red boy home, and his pack of dogs were delighted to see him. Their hearts raced happily as they rallied around their pack leader! However, it was as if they were celebrating guardedly, careful to not squish his fragile skinny body.

Clifford knew they were treating him cautiously, and he hobbled through them to grab a stinky sock. He stared at them with exhausted happiness as if to say, "Hey, everything is okay now. See, I am still the king of the socks!"

Cliff's eyes began to sleep, and the four dogs curled up together near Aunty Tammy's feet.

The moon started to bathe the ocean and tropical hillside with beams of blue, and the coconut trees twinkled with Christmas lights.

A gentle knock at the door slipped quietly into the room. It was Alyssa and her children, and they surprised Aunty Tammy with dinner.

Looking at each little face, all six children's eyes gleamed as they smiled about their accomplishment. Aunty Tammy's heart was overwhelmed and truly humbled, feeling blessed for *each* one of them.

Alyssa said, "We wanted to bring you dinner and tell you to rest now that your baby is home." It was the best food and the best rest with Clifford on her lap sleeping at *HOME!*

Moments later, Cliff noticed that Aunty Tammy was feeling such a mellow joy, and when their eyes locked, she had tears in her grateful eyes. She whispered, "Thank you, God, for my little ol' red miracle." He nuzzled onto her lap, pressing his fragile soft head to hers, reassuring her that everything was going to be okay. She petted his damp fur softly, and time stood sweetly still.

An endless blue and orange skyline embraced the quiet ocean.

Alyssa's family drove along the coastline singing "Joy to the World," their hearts full of love and sweet delight. Out of the car windows, they passed the twinkling lights while laughing and talking about Clifford's adventure. Each child shared a piece of the miraculous part they experienced. It was the most meaningful Christmas gift to witness all the kindness to rescue Clifford in a miraculous, heavenly-inspired group effort!

Tammy and Cliff

Owners found!

Tammy with Alyssa's family

Alyssa created Command Central in her living room with her six children, connecting the sister hikers and Aunty Tammy. Messages from all over America following this journey with prayers flow through the internet. With every disappointment there was more encouragement and courageous faith!

Little Ol' Red Miracle

CHAPTER 9

Christmas Week and Christmas Day

The family skipped the annual tradition of building Christmas sand castles at the beach. That could wait until next year, when Cliff could chase the sand crabs away from his family with his usual protective instincts. This year, they wanted nothing more than to celebrate the little ol' red miracle they just experienced.

Mila checked Clifford with her plastic doctor kit and said he looked great and that she was *happy* he was home. She could not stop hugging him.

Cliff loved all the sweetness and licked her little hands, appreciating her kindly caring for him.

Jetty pointed to what was left of Cliff's dog bed and placed a stinky sock in it as a welcome home gift.

Clifford breathed in the moment happily, almost smiling as they made cookies and gave him sweet hugs.

That week, the tree lights were hung, the nativity was lit, and the family enjoyed the little ornaments that much more. The incredible Christmas miracle added a special joy in their grateful hearts. It was a beautiful addition to another miracle for the family as they also welcomed their newest grandchild.

The End

Cliff, Tammy, Mila, and Jetty

Cliff

*Wailea, Ross, Hadu, Columbus, Cliff, and Tammy
in the back of their truck*

Mila and Cliff

Cliff, after the vet checkup

Cliff being rescued, the first time

Thank you for reading about my hopeful journey!
Always find faith, and He will guide you.

Merry Christmas!

— Little Ol' Red Miracle, Cliff

CLIFFORD'S UPDATE

Aunty Tammy took Clifford to see his veterinarian. The doctor and nursing staff were touched by the rescue story and checked him so sweetly. Thankfully, his tests came out good, and he only needed antibiotics for cuts and sores. His lungs were fine; however, he was only twenty-five pounds. The veterinarian provided a meal plan and care instructions to help Clifford heal and gain weight.

Luckily, Clifford had started treatment for fleas, ticks, and parasites two months earlier—we are all thankful that he had this protection during his twenty-one days wandering lost through the rain, on farms, in a waterfall and through the mountain.

Printed in the USA
CPSIA information can be obtained
at www.ICGtesting.com
CBHW050017161024
15911CB00001B/1

9 798893 330908